THIS BOOK BELONGS TO

....

....

HarperCollins
PUBLISHERS
Since 1817

™ & © Dr. Seuss Enterprises, L.P. 1997
All Rights Reserved

A CIP catalogue record for this title is available from
the British Library. No part of this publication may be
reproduced, stored in a retrieval system or transmitted in any
form or by any means, electronic, mechanical, photocopying, recording
or otherwise, without the prior permission of HarperCollins Publishers Ltd,
1 London Bridge Street, London SE1 9GF.

1 3 5 7 9 10 8 6 4 2

978-0-00-824165-0

www.harpercollins.co.uk

Printed and bound in China

Oh, Baby, the Places You'll Go!

Dr. Seuss

ADAPTED BY TISH RABE

HarperCollins *Children's Books*

Dear Reader,

My late husband, Theodor Geisel—known to most of you as "Dr. Seuss"—was intrigued by research into the development of babies while they are in their mother's womb. The fact that they could hear sounds—and might actually respond to the voices of their parents—was both exciting and mystifying to him.

Some years ago, Ted and I came across an article about some researchers who had asked prospective mothers and fathers to read aloud to their babies in utero. To our delight, the book they read was *The Cat in the Hat*. The researchers found increased uterine activity during the reading, and a gradual settling down afterward. This response to the book continued after delivery. The baby apparently recalled having heard the story before . . . *in utero!*

Ted loved his involvement in this bit of prenatal research.

This book is joyfully dedicated to Ted and to all you parents in the process of getting to know that most significant other (or others) . . . in utero.

Audrey Geisel
La Jolla, California

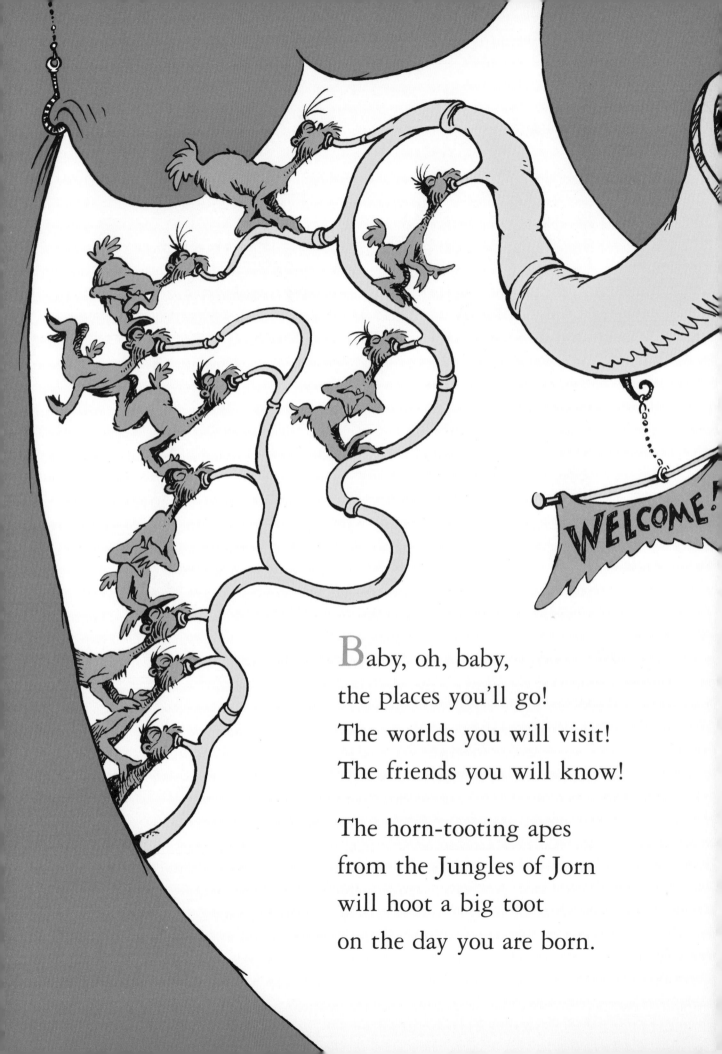

WELCOME!

Baby, oh, baby,
the places you'll go!
The worlds you will visit!
The friends you will know!

The horn-tooting apes
from the Jungles of Jorn
will hoot a big toot
on the day you are born.

While a bird flying high
from far off in Katroo
will sing on the wing,
"Happy Birthday to *you*!"

(Then the Once-ler will call
on his Whisper-ma-Phone
with a secret he's saving
for your ears alone.)

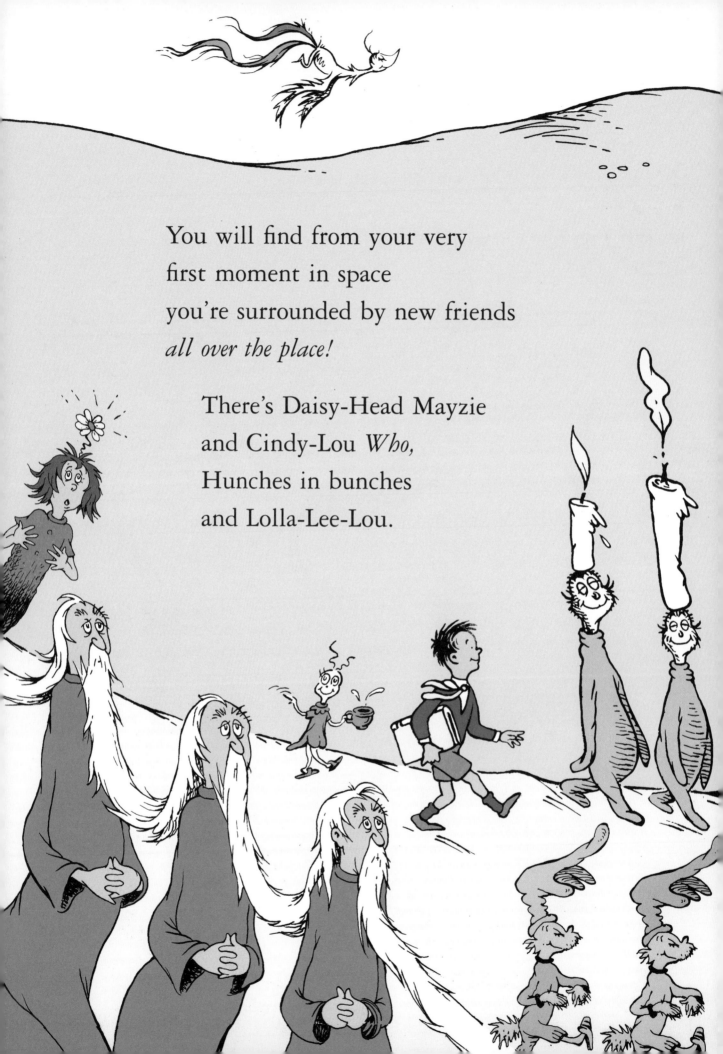

You will find from your very
first moment in space
you're surrounded by new friends
all over the place!

There's Daisy-Head Mayzie
and Cindy-Lou *Who,*
Hunches in bunches
and Lolla-Lee-Lou.

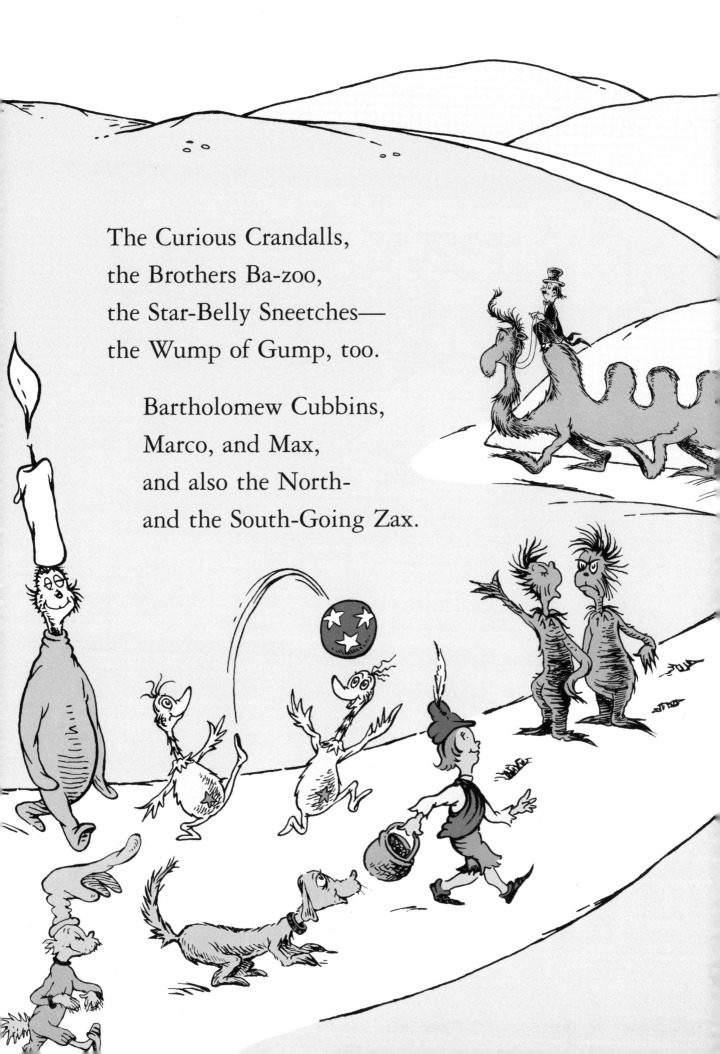

The Curious Crandalls,
the Brothers Ba-zoo,
the Star-Belly Sneetches—
the Wump of Gump, too.

Bartholomew Cubbins,
Marco, and Max,
and also the North-
and the South-Going Zax.

There's Thidwick, who lives
with his friends in a bunch
at a lake where there's lots
of sweet moose-moss to munch.

A very tall cat
in a red-and-white hat
who loves to do tricks
in West Gee-Hossa-Flat.

A boy with his yo-yo
(the youngest McCave)
and his 22 brothers,
who all are named Dave.

And a worm who can see
all the way to Japan,
which is quite a bit farther
than anyone can.

And Horton, who lives
in the Jungle of Nool,
every fifteenth of May
in the cool of the pool,
will show you the dust speck
that houses the *Whos,*
those brave little folks
we would not want to lose.
He saved their whole town,
for he knows, after all,
a person's a person,
no matter how small.

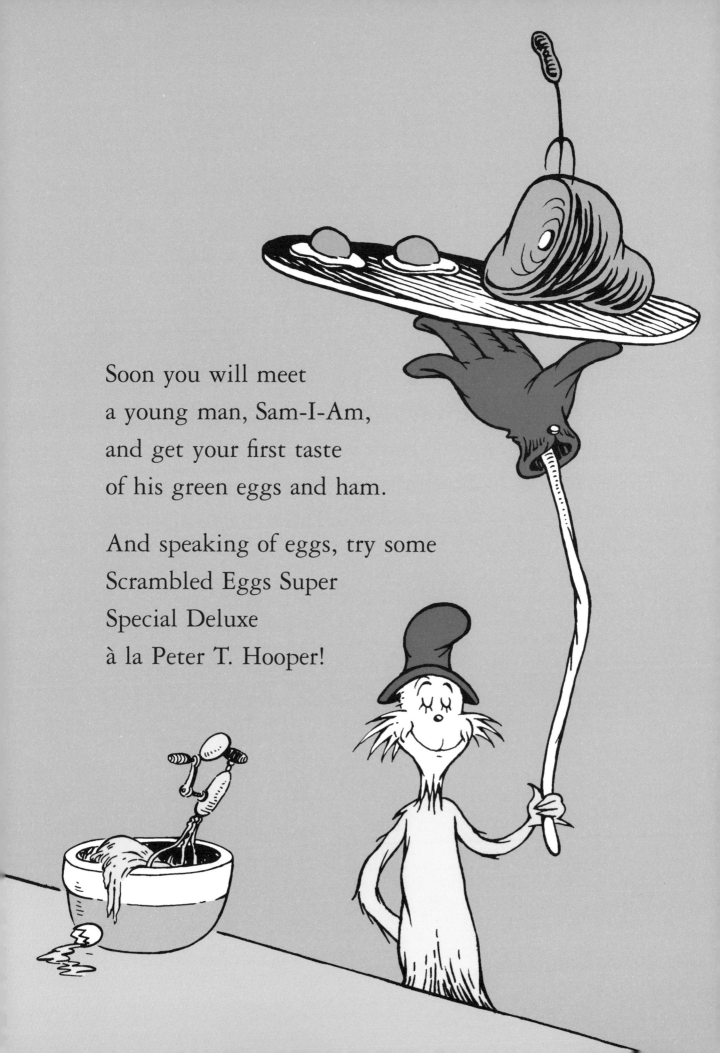

Soon you will meet
a young man, Sam-I-Am,
and get your first taste
of his green eggs and ham.

And speaking of eggs, try some
Scrambled Eggs Super
Special Deluxe
à la Peter T. Hooper!

You're also invited
to have some roast beast—
every Christmas in *Who*-ville,
it's really a feast.

You will visit great places
no speller can spell,
like the country of
Motta-fa-Potta-fa-Pell,
where you'll ride on a
Fizza-ma-Wizza-ma-Dill.
(You'd better do it, 'cause no one else will!)

Then take a quick trip
out to Sala-ma-Sond,
where Yertle the Turtle
was king of the pond,
till a turtle named Mack
did a plain little thing:
he burped . . .
and he toppled
the throne
of a king!

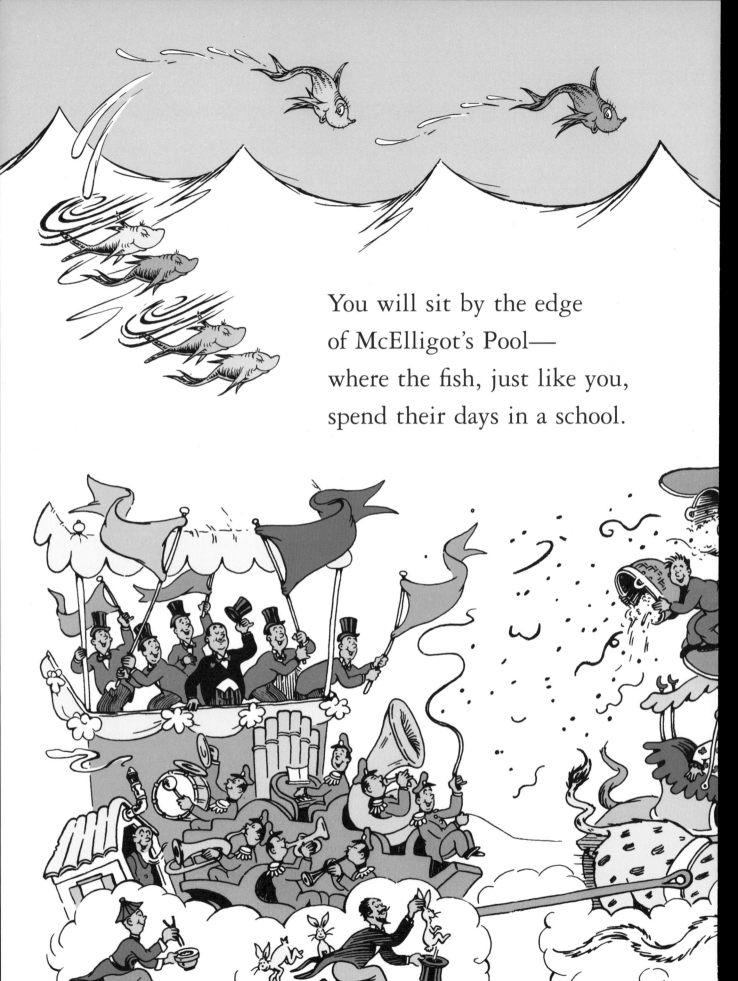

You will sit by the edge
of McElligot's Pool—
where the fish, just like you,
spend their days in a school.

And you'll find that it's fun
when you hop on your pop,
but don't be surprised
when he asks you to STOP!

On beyond Zebra,
you'll find a new letter,
like Yekk, Yuzz, or Wum,
that will make your life better.

And *you'll* have a story
that no one can beat
when you say that you saw it
on Mulberry Street.

But whatever you do,
things won't *always* go right.
You might meet the Grinch
in the dark of the night.
His heart is too small
and his shoes are too tight.
(He's not very friendly
and rarely polite.)

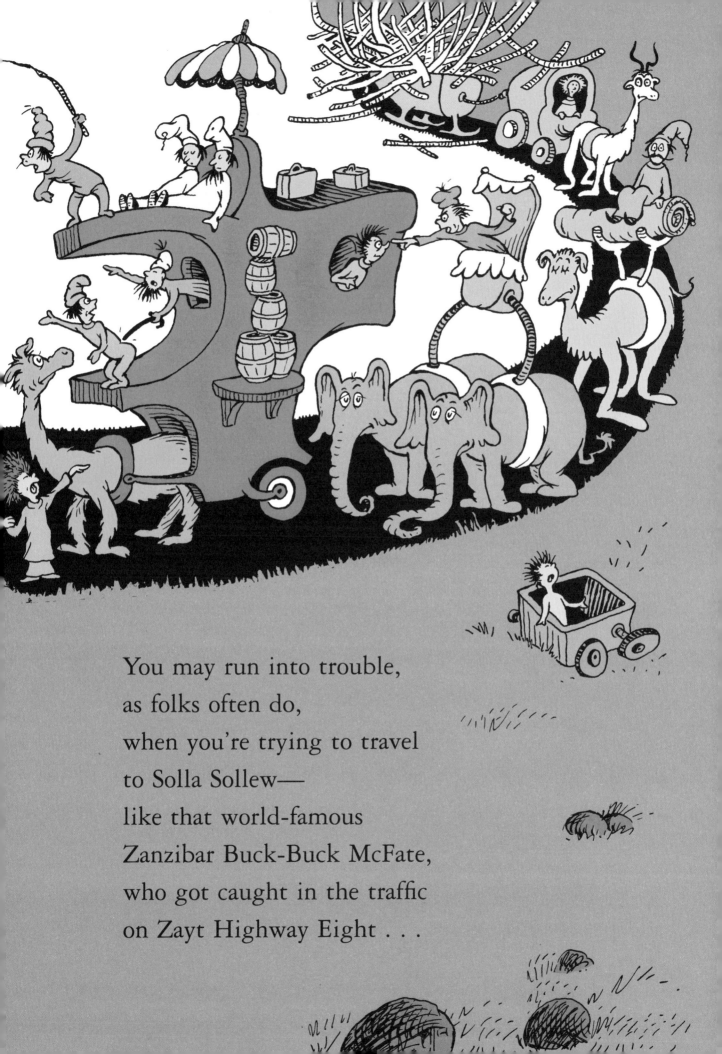

You may run into trouble,
as folks often do,
when you're trying to travel
to Solla Sollew—
like that world-famous
Zanzibar Buck-Buck McFate,
who got caught in the traffic
on Zayt Highway Eight . . .

While you are growing,
we're all busy counting
the days till we meet you—
excitement is mounting!

We've saved you a seat
at the first matinee
of the Circus McGurkus
(there are four every day),
where Great Daredevil Sneelock,
the world's bravest type,
will be pulled through the air
by three Soobrian Snipe
on a dingus contraption
attached to his pipe!

Here are two tickets
(for you and a guest)
to the new zoo, McGrew Zoo—
it's really the best.
It's there you will see
the great Russian Palooski.
This zoo, it is true,
has not one-ski, but two-ski.
Their headskis are redski;
their bellies are blueski.
(I'd try not to miss them, if I were you-ski!)

You'll find that this world's
a great place to begin,
but it *could* use some help—
which is where *you* come in.

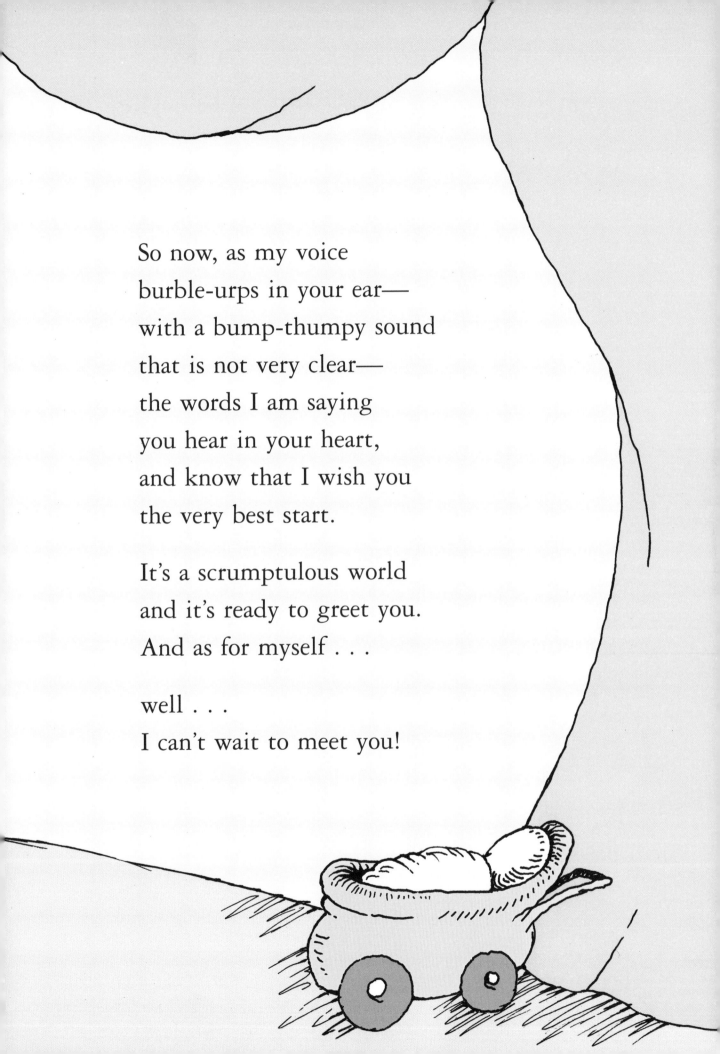

So now, as my voice
burble-urps in your ear—
with a bump-thumpy sound
that is not very clear—
the words I am saying
you hear in your heart,
and know that I wish you
the very best start.

It's a scrumptulous world
and it's ready to greet you.
And as for myself . . .

well . . .
I can't wait to meet you!

STORYBOOKS WRITTEN AND ILLUSTRATED BY DR. SEUSS

AND TO THINK THAT I SAW IT ON MULBERRY STREET
THE 500 HATS OF BARTHOLOMEW CUBBINS
THE KING'S STILTS
HORTON HATCHES THE EGG
McELLIGOT'S POOL
THIDWICK THE BIG-HEARTED MOOSE
BARTHOLOMEW AND THE OOBLECK
IF I RAN THE ZOO
SCRAMBLED EGGS SUPER!
HORTON HEARS A WHO!
ON BEYOND ZEBRA!
IF I RAN THE CIRCUS
HOW THE GRINCH STOLE CHRISTMAS!
YERTLE THE TURTLE AND OTHER STORIES
HAPPY BIRTHDAY TO YOU!
THE SNEETCHES AND OTHER STORIES
DR. SEUSS'S SLEEP BOOK
I HAD TROUBLE IN GETTING TO SOLLA SOLLEW
THE CAT IN THE HAT SONGBOOK
I CAN LICK 30 TIGERS TODAY! AND OTHER STORIES
I CAN DRAW IT MYSELF
THE LORAX
DID I EVER TELL YOU HOW LUCKY YOU ARE?
HUNCHES IN BUNCHES
THE BUTTER BATTLE BOOK
YOU'RE ONLY OLD ONCE!
OH, THE PLACES YOU'LL GO!
THE BIPPOLO SEED AND OTHER LOST STORIES
HORTON AND THE KWUGGERBUG AND MORE LOST STORIES
WHAT PET SHOULD I GET?

BEGINNER BOOKS WRITTEN AND ILLUSTRATED BY DR. SEUSS

THE CAT IN THE HAT
THE CAT IN THE HAT COMES BACK
ONE FISH TWO FISH RED FISH BLUE FISH
GREEN EGGS AND HAM
HOP ON POP
DR. SEUSS'S ABC
FOX IN SOCKS
THE FOOT BOOK
MR. BROWN CAN MOO! CAN YOU?
MARVIN K. MOONEY WILL YOU PLEASE GO NOW!
THE SHAPE OF ME AND OTHER STUFF
THERE'S A WOCKET IN MY POCKET!
OH, THE THINKS YOU CAN THINK!
THE CAT'S QUIZZER
I CAN READ WITH MY EYES SHUT!
OH SAY CAN YOU SAY?

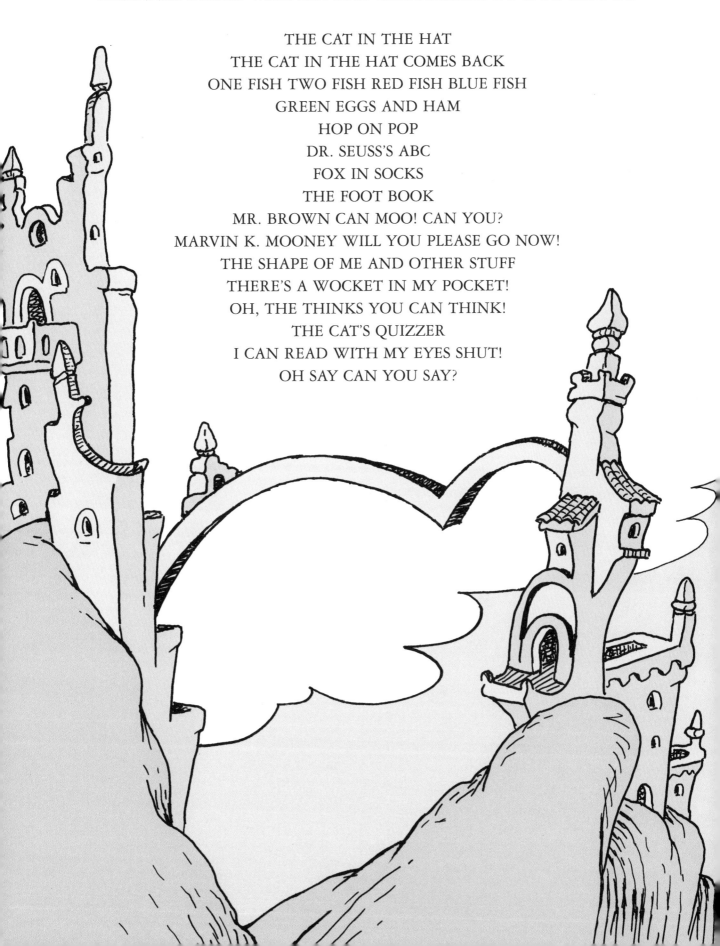